FROM CASTS
to comics

Cat Jenkins
James Quinton

From Casts to Comics

CAT JENKINS
JAMES QUINTON

Storyshares

Storyshares
Storyshares, LLC
24 N. Bryn Mawr Avenue #340
Bryn Mawr, PA 19010-3304

www.storyshares.org

Aligned with the Science of Reading.

Interest Level: 4th grade and beyond

9798885976534

Book design by Storyshares

A Storyshares Decodables Chapter Book

TABLE OF CONTENTS

MAX
Picks Up A Pen

CAT JENKINS

Max Picks Up a Pen

CAT JENKINS

"Max Picks Up A Pen"

short vowels: a, i, e

short a

Max	class
ball	patted
had	travel
bad	sat
mad	ask
sad	batted
cat	

short e

test	better	end
red	extra	letters
felt	credit	penpal
Met	yell	met
best	get	help
bed	credit	end
get	tell	desk
		sketch

short i

win	picked	ticket
hits	fishing	still
Biff	did	did
ships	pic	it
timber	in	fish
kicked	will	Flick
his	city	

high frequency words

was	you	them
were	they	but
when	more	could
that	some	
with	here	

challenge words

Seattle	person
school	history
marks	wrote
comic	write
model	extra
	travel

@storyshares.org

Max wanted to yell.

"No basketball," say Mom and Dad.

"No basketball," says Ms. Ana.

"To play ball, you have to do well in class," they add.

But in class, it was bad.

The red D on his test
looked as mad as Max felt.

He wanted a ball in
his hands. Not a pen.

Max is a Met.

The Mets are the best kids' ball team in Seattle.

Max *has* to help the Mets get a win in 2023.

When Max has the ball, he is at his tops.

Max is one of the best Mets. When Max is hot, he hits all of his shots.

Max **can not** get kicked off the Mets.

Max sat on his bed with his cat, Biff.

"What am I going to do, Biff?
I have to get help in class."

Max looked at his comics, and his
car mags. They did not help.

Mom said, "Ask Mr. Flick."

Dad said, "I bet Mr. Flick can help."

So Max did. He asked Mr. Flick.

Mr. Flick said, "You can get extra credit, Max."

"You can be part of LEX, with a penpal," added Mr. Flick.

"LEX stands for letter exchange. You write letters to a penpal for extra credit in this class. So you can pass."

Max was not sure.

He did not like to read.

He did not like to write.

But Max had to be on the Mets.
He *had* to play ball.

Max sat at his desk. He got his pen.

It was hard! To write to someone he had never met.

"What do I write, Biff?"

Biff batted his paw.

"I am from Seattle. I will tell my penpal that."

Max wrote of his city. Of the ships, timber, and fish. He wrote that he likes Bball, comics, and cars. But NOT class.

At the end, he sketched a pic of Biff.

Dear penpal,

My city has a history of ships, travel, timber, and fishing.

In my city, I like basketball, and comics with pictures, and cars.

I do not like reading or school.

Your pal,
Max

It was one letter, but Max felt glad.

Max could play ball. Now that he had a penpal.

MIN'S UNLIKELY PENPAL

JAMES QUINTON

"Min's Unlikely Penpal"

short vowels: a, i, e

short a

sat	Ba	basketball
at	dad	class
tap	had	cat
Saturday	pal	patted
last	Max	back
	asked	added
	glad	flag
	that	

short (e)

her	exchange
desk	LEX
get	send
letter	penpals
yelled	help
red	went
well	best
upset	pens

short i

Min	comic
it	kids
into	Biff
this	him
is	with
did	filled
until	grinned

high frequency words

the	what	friends	know
of	would	from	out
was	new	why	those
said	world	want	first
move	now	how	about
done	does	to	

challenge words

wheelchair	paint
confused	dumplings
writing	Chinese
connect	smiled

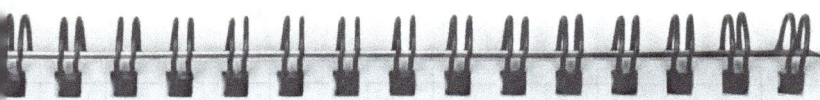
Min sat at her desk.

Her hands tap-tap-tapped on the arms of her wheelchair.

It was Saturday. Her last day to get a letter this week.

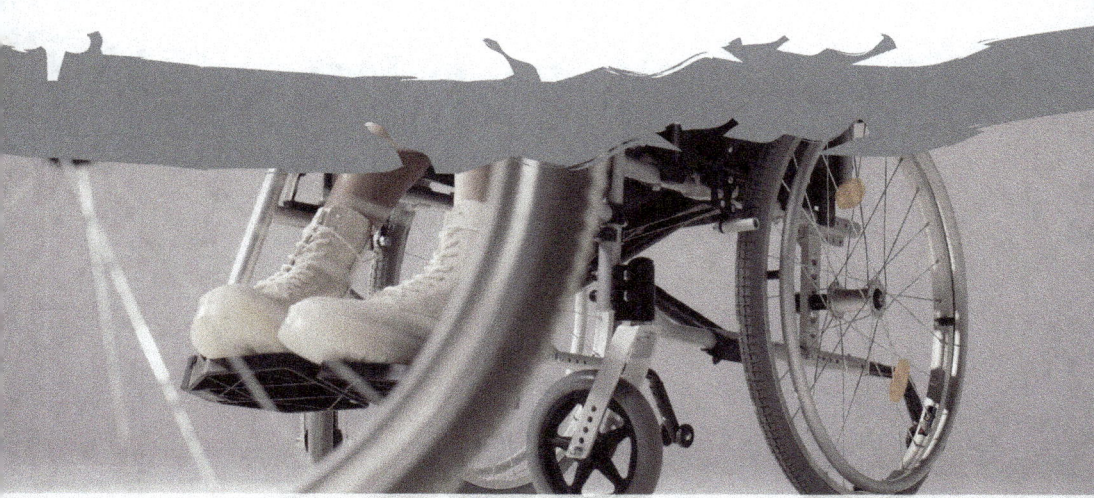

"Min, it is here!" her Ba yelled.

Min turned her wheels. Her dad ran into her room.

He had a red letter.

"Open it," Ba said. Min did.

Ba did not move until Min was done reading.

"Well?" he asked.

Min was... *what? Glad? Upset?*

Confused. Min was confused.

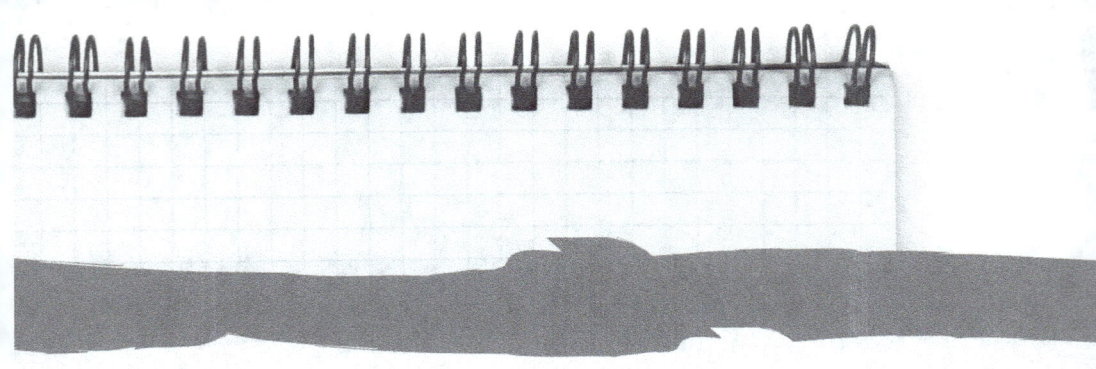

LEX said that she would get a new penpal.

LEX = Letter Exchange.

A way for kids to send letters, with penpals.

Min had new friends all over the world from LEX.

She had waited for days to get a letter from her new penpal.

But now...

"His name is Max," she said to her dad. "From Seattle. He likes comics and cars and basketball.

But he does not like to read. Or class. Or writing! Why would Max want to be in LEX?"

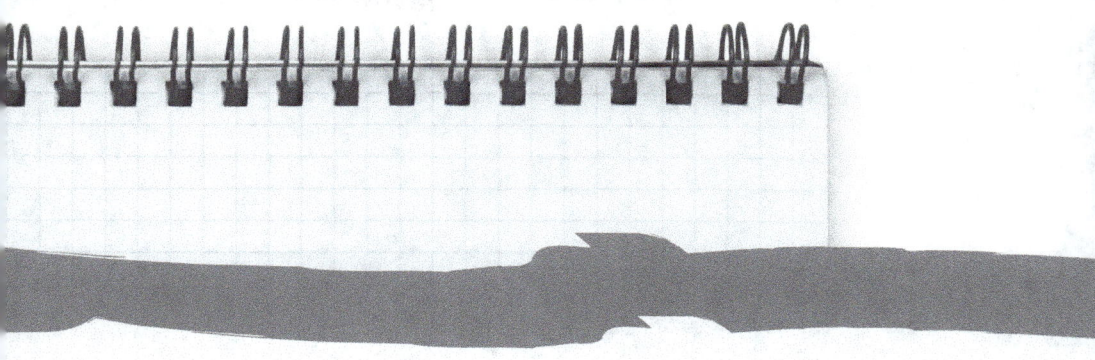

Min's dad did not say a word. He liked to think first.

"Max does like to read," Ba said at last. "He reads comics. He also likes to sketch. See?"

Ba put his finger on a drawing of Max's cat, Biff. "Do you see how the two connect?"

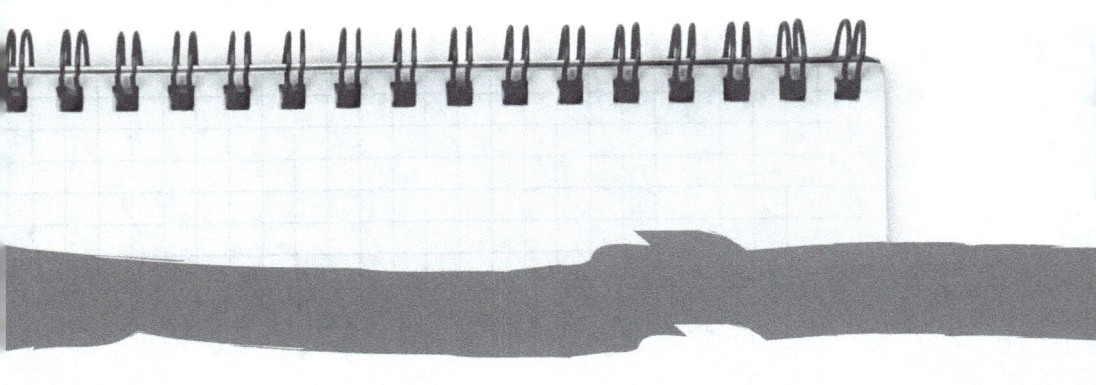

Min did not get it.

"He likes art!" Ba said. "He likes books with art and letters with art.

And I know an artist."

Ba winked. He patted Min on the back.

"You can help him to love reading, and writing, and class. Talk to him with your art."

Her dad was right!

Min went back to her desk. She got out her best brushes and pens. She began.

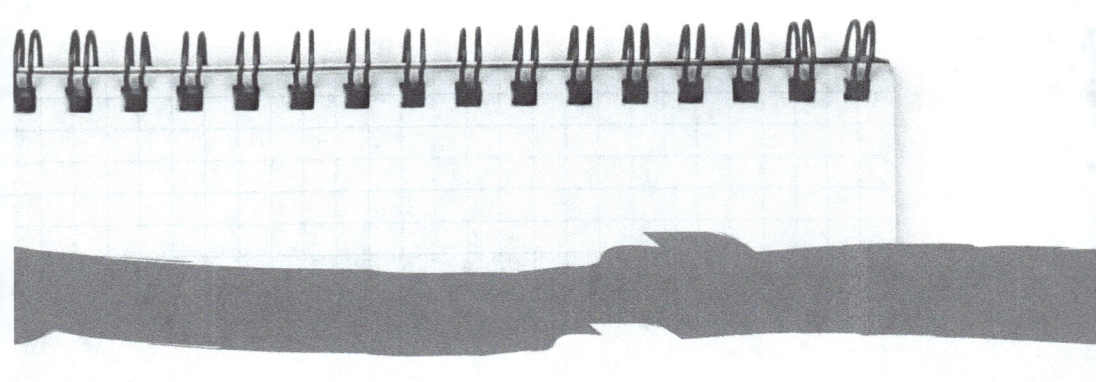

First, a short comic for Max about her life. It was filled with pictures of books and art.

She added her wheels. And her desk. She painted a flag. That was for her home, Australia.

She drew dumplings. Those were for her Chinese history. She drew Ba.

Last, she drew a basketball.

That was for Max. Her new penpal.

She grinned.

This may be the start of something great.

A Shock for
MAX

CAT JENKINS

A SHOCK
FOR MAX

CAT JENKINS

"A Shock for Max"

short vowel: o

rt o

shock	rock	not	fox
lost	sock	top	got
blob	doctor	stop	hot
on	clop	comics	dogs
log	off	job	flock
block	plopped	hop	mocked
shot	drop	cross	long
pop	sob	jock	forgot

high frequency words

work	thought
for	walk
so	loved
could	were
the	right
was	good
out	about
would	okay
now	month
no	
wanted	

challenge words

ankle	kangaroos
swelled	koala
lump	writing
season	
wrote	

@storyshares.org

3

*M*ax felt lost.

He sat like a blob on a log while the Mets played basketball.

All that work for a penpal so he could stay on the team.

Then Max went to block a shot and felt a pop.

His ankle swelled up. The lump was like a rock under his sock.

The doctor told Max to sit out the season. Max would have to clop about with a cast on his shin.

No more Mets. He was off the team. Max was in shock.

He plopped down on his bed and let his head drop.

Max wanted to sob, but it was not that bad.

He would be back on top in a month or so.

Max thought of his penpal, Min.

Min was in a wheelchair and could not walk at all.

But Min was kind and happy and did not let it stop her.

And she wrote the best letters.

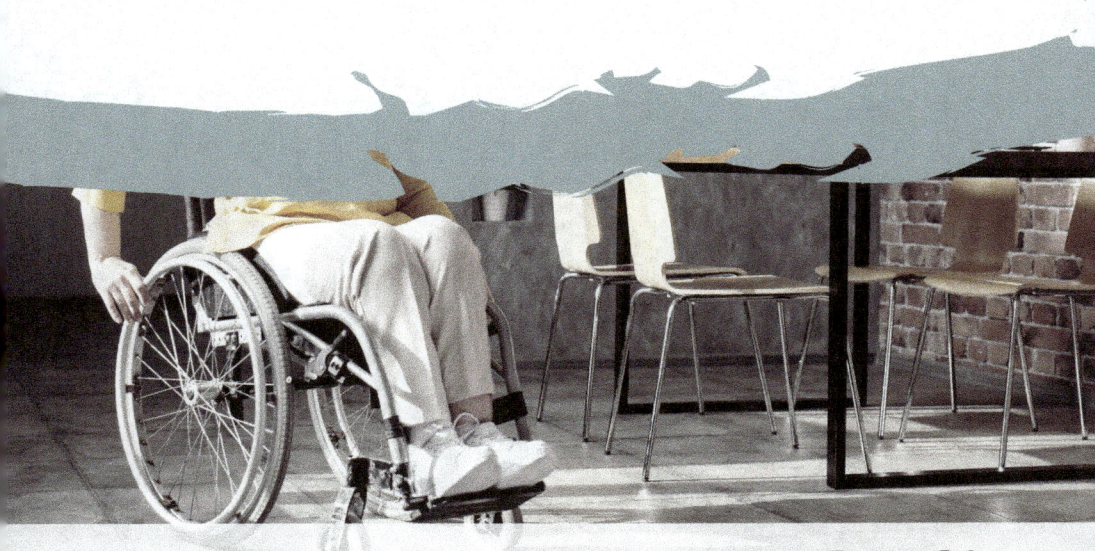

Max loved the letters he got from Min.

They were like comics that made reading fun, not a job.

Max took out his last comic from Min.

Her drawings made him grin.

But then his grin went dim.

If it made Max sad to hop about with a cast, how did Min feel?

Did anyone send Min comic-letters to help when she was cross?

Max's slow smile came back. "Maybe I'm not a jock right now, but I can be a good pal."

Max picked up a pen and began to draw.

Min had kangaroos and koala bears.

Max bet she would love Seattle animals.

Dear Min,

This is a fox that was in my yard. It got into the trash looking for hot dogs.

And this is my cat, Biff, and a flock of birds that mocked him!

Your pal,
Max

Before long, Max forgot he was not playing basketball.

Learning about Min and her home was fun.

Telling Min about his life was fun. And drawing was fun too.

Maybe...reading and writing were not so bad.

Maybe...learning was okay too.

Max was in shock.

But in a good way this time.

MIN LIFTS UP MAX

CAT JENKINS

"Min Lifts Up Max"

short vowel: u

short u

hum	hugged	uncle
begun	tugged	bubbles
shut	pulled	trucks
hung	up	fun
jumped	support	plucked
buses	under	luck

high frequency words

challenge words

opened	family	use
love	would	other
year	here	could
where	every	mean
from	into	you
their	during	your

envelope	weather
favorite	ankle
businesses	bubbles
signs	drawers
Australia	bright
rolled	celebration

$\mathcal{M}$in opened her eyes.

She sat up. She blinked.

There was a red envelope on her desk.

"Love, Ba" was written on top.

Min started to hum.

The envelope meant that Golden Week had begun.

It was her favorite week of the year.

国庆节

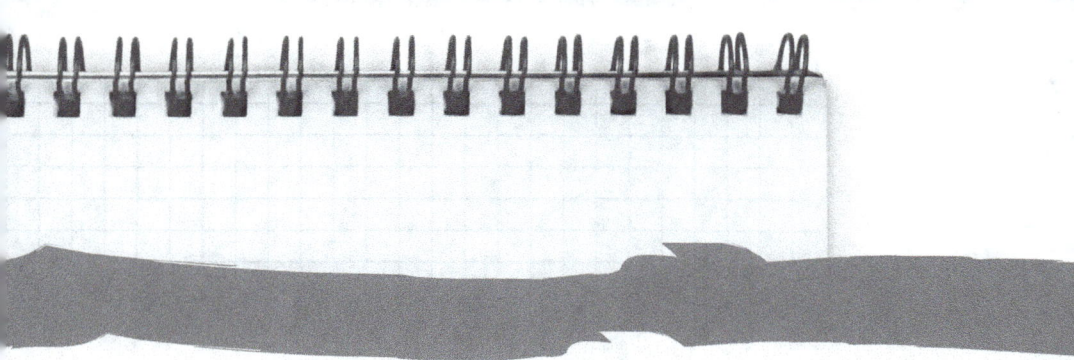

Golden Week was a time for rest.

For family.

It was a time of dance.

And song.

And color.

Golden Week started in China.

That's where her family was from.

For 7 days, schools shut their doors.

Businesses hung "closed" signs.

Many people hurried onto trains.
And planes.

Others jumped into cars and
buses.

All of them were off to be with
family.

Min hugged herself.

Her family would be here soon.

They visited Australia to be with her and her dad every year at this time.

Min tugged off her blankets.

She pulled herself into her wheelchair. Then she rolled to her desk.

The red envelope held bills. They were for her to spend during Golden Week.

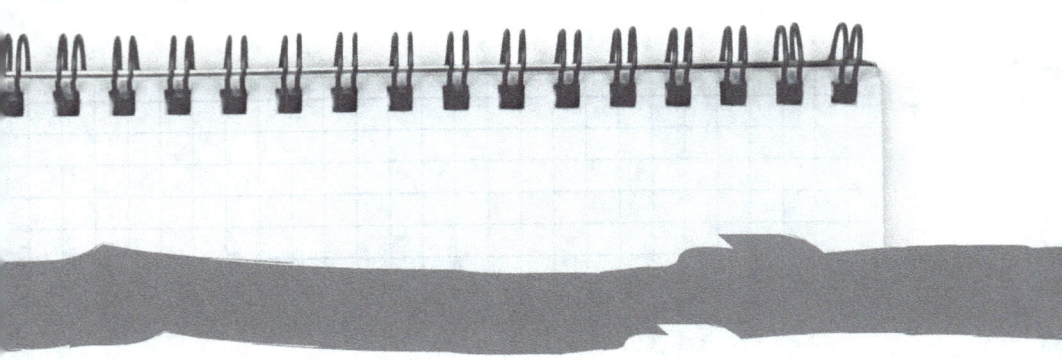

She liked to use them to buy art.

Many Chinese artists set up tables to shop at in town.

Min loved to support other artists.

This year would be a little different.

This time, she would buy art to send to Max.

Max was feeling under the weather.

He had a broken ankle.

This meant he could not play basketball.

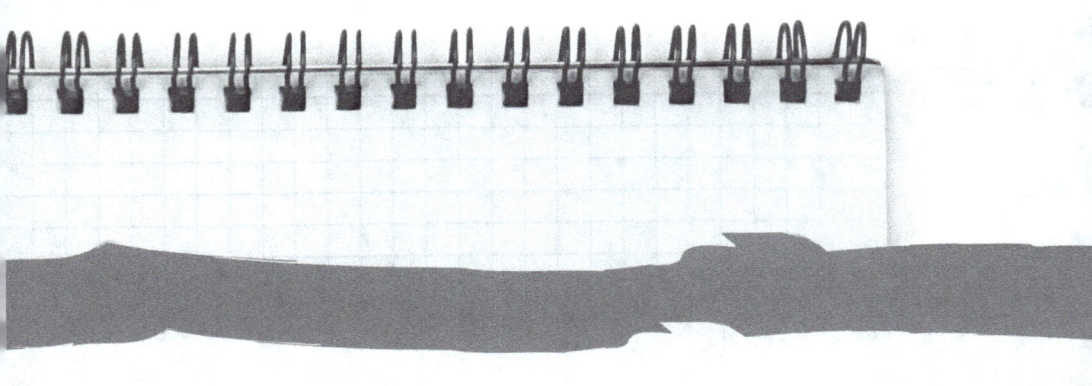

Min opened her desk drawers.

She pulled out 5 paintings she had made.

One was for her aunt. Another was for her uncle.

And three were for her cousins.

Ba was already on his way to pick them up.

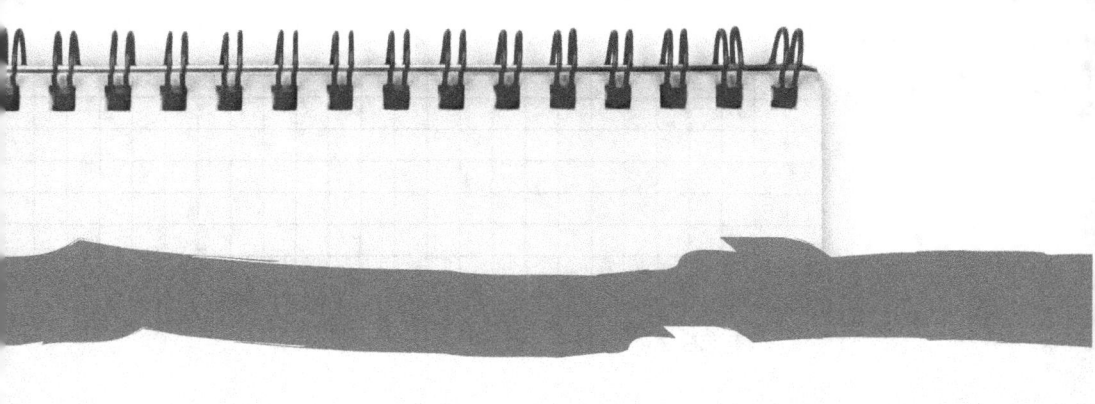

Min had one other thing to get ready.

She got a blank paper.

She drew lines and bubbles on it.

Later, she would add pictures.

It was going to be a comic for Max about Golden Week.

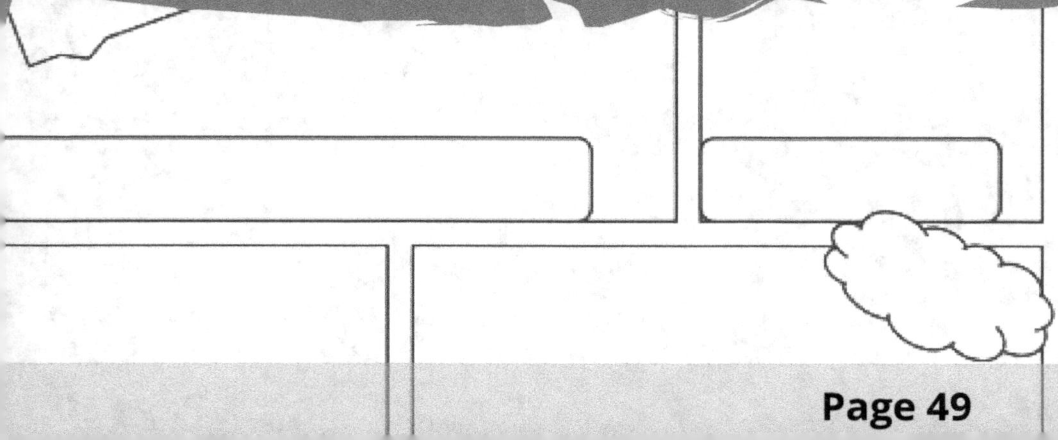

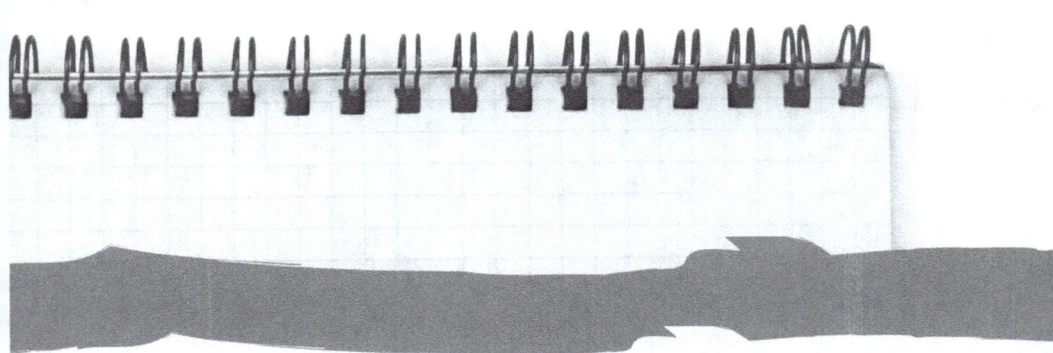

At last, Min heard the hum of Ba's car.

Soon, she was covered in hugs and kisses.

Her family was loud and bright. Like the paintings she gave to them.

They were all dressed in red. It was the color of celebration.

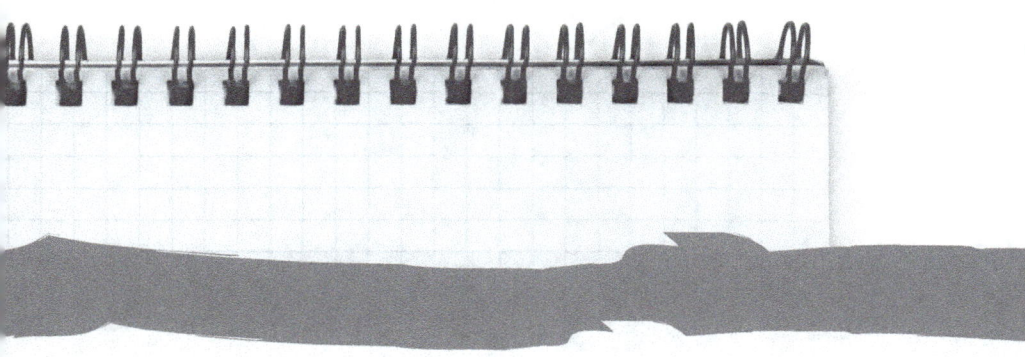

Together, they all went to the city.

There were lanterns up and down the streets.

There were food trucks. And a fun parade.

Ba rolled Min from art table to art table.

At last, she plucked up the perfect piece.

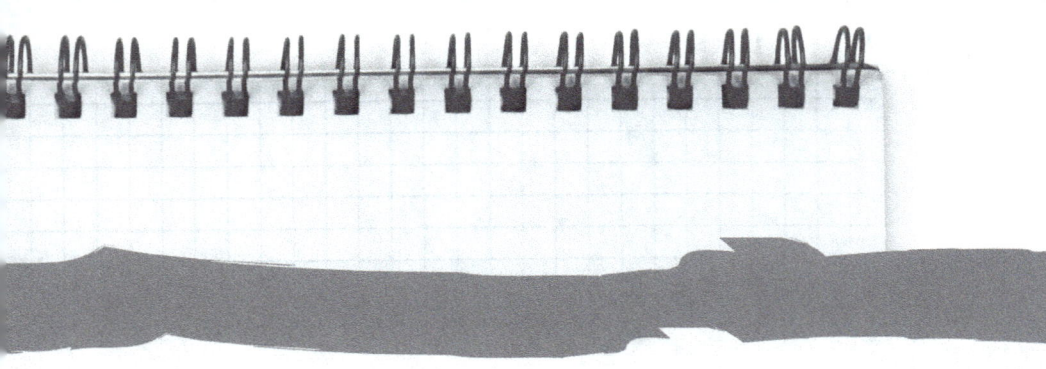

It was a panda, painted red and gold. The colors of Max's basketball team!

Pandas mean friendship. And helping a hurt panda was good luck.

Min hoped this gift would lift Max up.

That would be good luck for them both.

- *Your pal, Min*

About the Authors

Cat Jenkins lives in the Pacific Northwest where the weather is often conducive to long hours before a keyboard. Her stories in humor, fantasy, speculative fiction, and horror have been published both online and in print. Her first novel, *Sara When She Chooses,* was published by Bedazzled Ink Publishing in May 2018. Cat's blog can be found at: catjenkinsdotcom.wordpress.com.

James Quinton is a writer from a small town in central Massachusetts. When he's not at his desk, he's either in his garden coaxing his plants to grow or in his workshop turning salvaged wood and flea market finds into one-of-a-kind furniture and home decor.

www.ingramcontent.com/pod-product-compliance
Lightning Source LLC
Chambersburg PA
CBHW071402260526
45589CB00082B/592